Thursday

	Andrea	Jonathan
Literature	p. 20-30 The Prince and the Pauper	Pilgrim's Progress chapter 2. 16-22
Grammar	p.7-8 Capitalization	p. 6-8 Capitalization
Math	lesson ... Negative Exponents	lesson 32 Rounding off whole numbers
Vocabulary	Ex.	lesson 5 Exercise A
History	p. 18-22 Spanish ... Explorations	p. 191-194 European Beginnings
Science	Stream B...	Stream Biology

	Em...	Susanna
...ding	Read Around the World p. 12-13	Coloring pages 8-9
	p. 4-5 good se...	Nu...
	addition, flash...ds	Let...
	...opy words	St...
	Aa	
	...ears of Discovery p 9-14	
	...tream... - at the creek	

Red Oak

Beec...

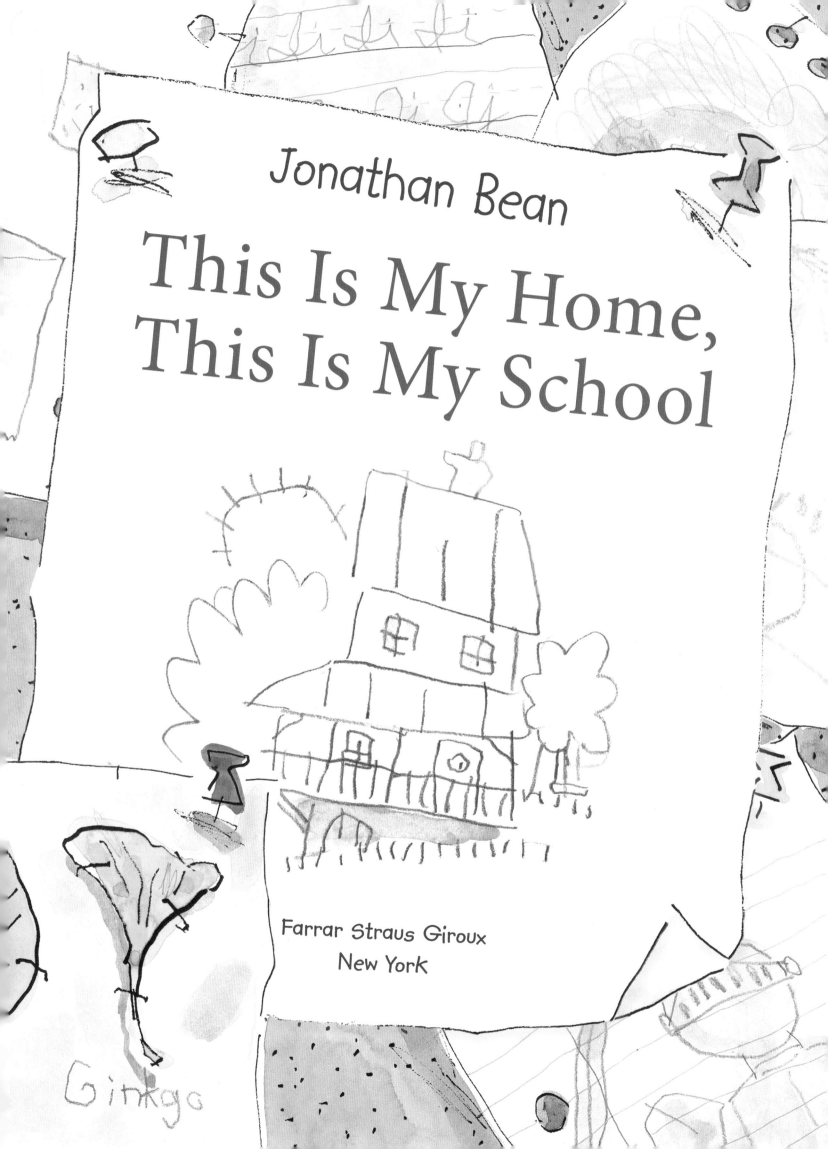

Jonathan Bean

This Is My Home, This Is My School

Farrar Straus Giroux
New York

Ginkgo

Farrar Straus Giroux Books for Young Readers
175 Fifth Avenue, New York 10010

Copyright © 2015 by Jonathan Bean
All rights reserved
Color separations by Bright Arts (H.K.) Ltd.
Printed in China by Toppan Leefung Printing Ltd.,
Dongguan City, Guangdong Province
First edition, 2015
1 3 5 7 9 10 8 6 4 2

mackids.com

Library of Congress Cataloging-in-Publication Data
Bean, Jonathan, 1979– author, illustrator.
This is my home, this is my school / Jonathan Bean. — First edition.
    pages cm
    Summary: "The boy from BUILDING OUR HOUSE takes us through a typically
boisterous homeschooling day with his big family"—Provided by publisher.
    ISBN 978-0-374-38020-5 (hardback)
    [1. Home schooling—Fiction.   2. Family life—Fiction.]   I. Title.

PZ7.B3664Thi 2015
[E]—dc23
                                                                          2014040682

Farrar Straus Giroux Books for Young Readers may be purchased for business or promotional use.
For information on bulk purchases please contact Macmillan Corporate and Premium Sales Department
at (800) 221-7945 x5442 or by email at specialmarkets@macmillan.com.

For my parents, who built a
house then formed a school
—J.B.

This is my home.

And *this* is my school!

What, confused? Okay, allow me to explain.

See, this is my mom and my sisters.

And these are my classmates and my teacher. Follow us!

This is our classroom.

This is another one of our classrooms.

And this.

This, too!

We have a lot of classrooms.

And this is our cafeteria.

Watch out,
here comes the crabby cafeteria lady!

We have a big playground.

But there's nowhere the school bully can't find you.

He's such a beast!

Of course, we have a trusty school bus.

It's always ready to take us to . . .

the library.

Or . . .

on field trips!

This is our art room.

This is the world!

Sometimes our teacher
gets tired very easily.

Oh no, she's calling for help!

This is the *substitute* teacher.

This is our dad!

It's time for shop class.

Then the sub helps us with our homework.

And when our school gets lots of visitors . . .

he leads phys ed!

I guess sometimes the students get tired easily, too.

This is show-and-tell . . .

and our dinner.

Our astronomy class . . .

and our English lesson.

Friday

	Andrea	Jonathan
Literature		Pilgrim's Progress Chapters 3, p. 22-30
Grammar		p. 9-10 Capitalization
Math		lesson 4 Austrian Subtraction
Vocabulary	Ex. 3-c	lesson 5 Exercise B
History	P. 22-30 French ...	P. 194-199 European Beginnings
Science	stream ...	Finish work from stream field trip

	Emily	Susanna
...ding	Read Around the ... P. 14-15	Coloring p... 10-11
	p. 5-6 good senta...	Num
	subtraction) flash cards	Lette
	...y words	Make
	..., Bb	
	...rs of Dictionary P. 15-17	
	Fini... work from ...trip	

Big Dipper

Sttrea...
dragonfly
eggs
nymph

Because this is my home,
this is my school.

Author's Note

Homeschooling never ends. When I called up my dad to check a chemical equation that I had pulled off the Internet for one of my pictures, he pointed out a couple of flaws and then launched into an explanation that put me right back in the position of the student who saved his most difficult chemistry and math problems for when his dad got home from work. Home and work, work and school, school and home were all seamlessly connected by my parents' curiosity to learn and teach. In Pennsylvania, where my sisters and I were homeschooled, students were required to assemble a portfolio to represent the year's learning. This turned homeschoolers into scavengers. "Take it for the portfolio" was our mantra, and no pamphlet or photogenic moment was safe. It was something of a joke even then, but it represented my parents' approach to school: no moment, whether at desk, dinner table, stream, play, or work, was too insignificant to be scavenged for something to learn.

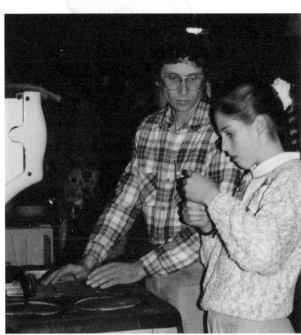